D1245096

For

Chelsea, Matthew, Sarah, our world.

Nola and Julian —
May your days be filled
with stories of hope and
your nights with sweet
dreams!

Tim Hale

Molly and Magruder missed their city just like all the other red-winged blackbirds from New York.

In fact, everyone they knew missed the hustle and bustle of New York City, but when the people started to leave because they were afraid of catching the virus, Molly and Magruder flew up the Hudson River.

While Molly, Magruder, and many of their friends enjoyed spending time in the Hudson Valley, fluttering through the open fields, chasing rolling streams, and particularly visiting apple orchards on sunny summer afternoons, there was nothing like the excitement of New York City.

Molly and Magruder often
talked about how they would wave
their wings as their friend, Ryder,
would scoot across the foot bridge over
the West Side Highway on his way to
school on Wall Street each morning.

"Remember how swiftly we had to flap
our wings to keep up?" chuckled
Magruder. "Yes, but it was good
exercise," responded Molly.

It was good exercise for Ryder's

mommy too as she jogged

alongside, pushing River, Ryder's

little brother, in a stroller.

Surely River must be walking by now,

Molly thought.

After waving goodbye to the boys, the two birds would often perch on the railing of a ferry gliding up the East River to midtown.

From there they would fly to

one of their favorite spots,

right on the nose of a lion

statue in front of the

New York Public Library.

Then they would have a

leisurely lunch in Bryant Park

amongst the yogis, coffee

drinkers, and ping-pong players.

Quite a few months passed since they flew to the Hudson Valley and, just in time for the flowers and trees to bloom, Molly and Magruder felt it was safe enough to return to the city.

They were certain their fellow New Yorkers were ready to head back as well.

They hovered above some neighborhoods they hadn't spent much time in before, grinning as they passed the Cloisters, Washington Heights, and Columbia University.

Molly and Magruder were delighted to see people filling the streets again.

Their first stop was Central Park. As they turned off Fifth Avenue, they saw a line of people waiting to get into the Metropolitan Museum.

"The Met must be open again," cheered Molly. "This is a good sign."

Magruder assured Molly, "The city is coming back to life again. I knew it would!"

Molly and Magruder flitted over the

Boat Basin where Magruder dipped

and darted past people rowing slowly

around the lake, then to the Bethesda

Terrace, where Molly flew in circles,

popping into the background as

people took selfies.

Both red-winged blackbirds were ecstatic when they saw families entering the Children's Zoo. They hovered over the sea lions just long enough to notice that all the people were wearing face coverings.

"Good idea," said Molly. "They can have fun while staying safe and healthy."

They were so happy they barely noticed a light rain beginning to fall. "No problem," said Magruder, "Let's head over to Belvedere Castle." They waited patiently in the castle's turret, listening to the echoing raindrops until the sun began to shine again.

Next, they zipped over to the Great

Lawn filled with picnickers. Everyone's

blankets were carefully placed six feet

apart on all sides.

"I wonder if the New York City Ballet will have their spring season," pondered Molly. Magruder suggested they fly over to Lincoln Center to find out. Gathering around the fountain were bands of ballerinas, practicing their pliés as they talked. "Another good sign," Magruder said, "Let's go see what's going on in the theater district too."

The birds flew south.

Feeling hopeful when they saw words filling the marquees all around Times Square, Molly and Magruder continued on to the heart of Greenwich Village. The streets were filled with people, but some stores remained closed. This made Molly a bit sad. "Look!" Magruder pointed his wing, "So many restaurants still have outdoor seating. Remember that one? I think they really have the best spaghetti in the city!"

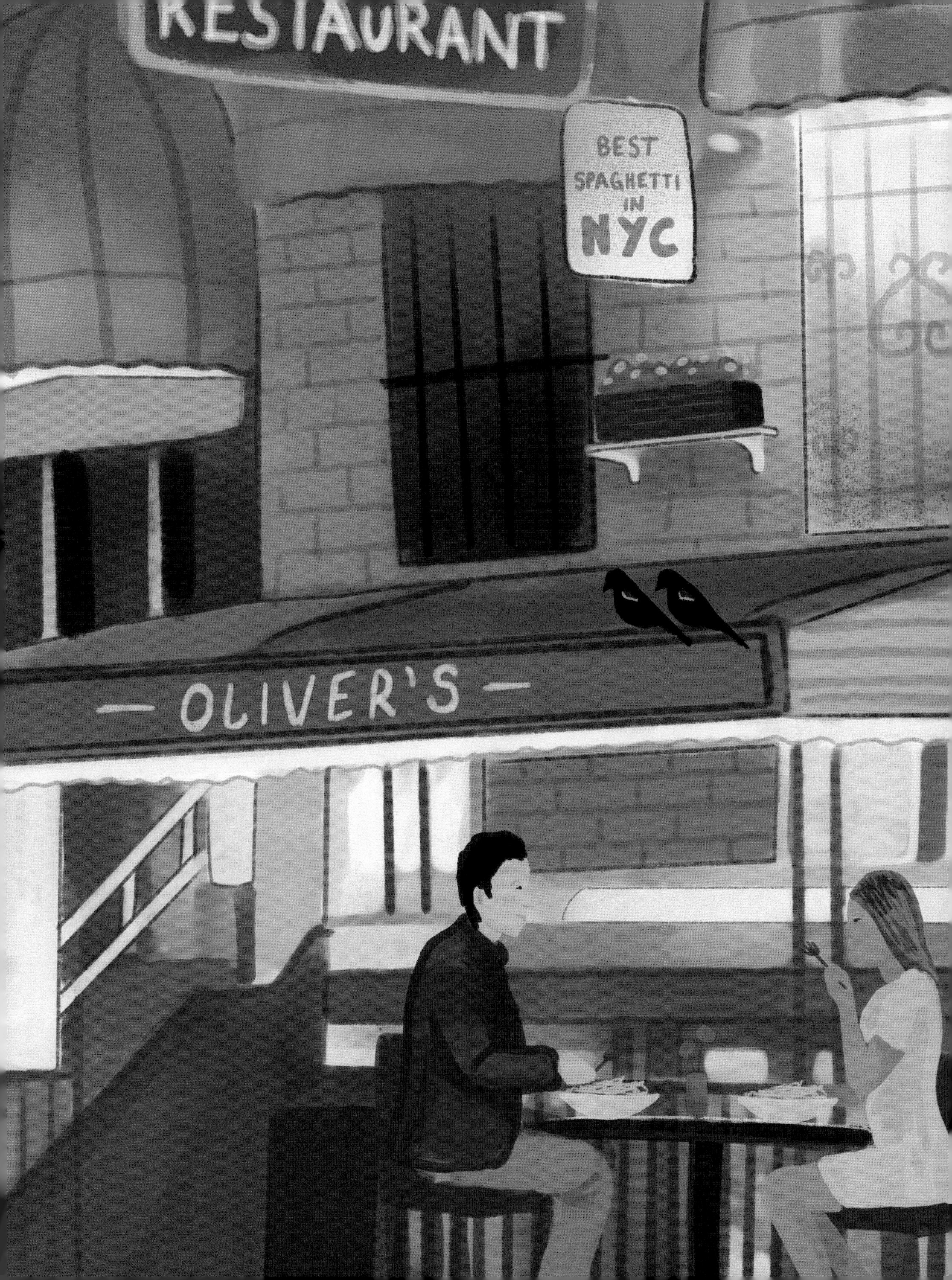
RESTAURANT
BEST SPAGHETTI IN NYC
— OLIVER'S —

Magruder encouraged Molly, "Keep flying. Soon we'll be in Washington Square Park." He knew she loved the park and hoped to find more signs of activity in the city they missed while they were up in the Hudson Valley.

They instantly heard music filling the air as they flew under the arch into Washington Square Park. Children skipped around the fountain, college students walked to classes, and their favorite pianist played some jazzy songs. New York was undoubtedly coming back to life.

Molly and Magruder were joyful at the sight of all the people back in the city, but they also felt confused because everywhere they went, people wore face coverings that disguised their expressions. "How do we know if they are smiling?" Molly asked Magruder. The two red-winged blackbirds sat on the top branch of their favorite English Elm, where they had a perfect view of all the passing people.

Suddenly, Molly realized that if she watched people's eyes, she could see them twinkle when they smiled. Molly directed her wing toward a group of children running up and down the green asphalt hills. Laughter filled the air. "Can you see how their eyes sparkle, Magruder? They are happy! I think they are smiling under those face coverings."

Seeing all the twinkling eyes made

Molly wonder if Ryder and

River had returned to New York City

too. Magruder suggested they head

downtown to find out. The two

red-winged blackbirds found a

comfortable bush across from the boys'

building and settled in for the evening.

Even after the sun went down, they continued to watch people, but didn't see Ryder and River. Magruder began to feel blue, but Molly reminded him of all the great things they had seen that day. "New York will be more exciting than ever," she told Magruder. They talked about how the children played in the park, how the streets were filled with people, and how the picnickers sat six feet apart.

Best of all, they learned to

recognize a smile through the gleam

in people's eyes, even when a mask

covered part of their face. Finally, the

birds rested.

The morning sun dancing in the reflection of the tall buildings awakened Molly and Magruder. They stretched their wings and looked up to see the shade going up in Ryder and River's bedroom window.

Shortly, two little boys that certainly resembled Ryder and River came charging through the front door of the building. "Look Molly, that boy seems quite tall for Ryder. What do you think?" asked Magruder. Molly looked carefully. "The smaller one is not just walking; he is trying to run. Let's follow them." The birds followed the family to the park that overlooked the Statue of Liberty; the whole time, studying the boys, wondering if they were their old friends.

The birds perched just a few feet away from the family. Suddenly, River pointed at Molly and Magruder and shouted, "Birdie, birdie!" They all turned to see. "Look, the red-winged blackbirds came back to the city too, Mommy!" Ryder cheered.

"Of course, they did. New York is their home too," explained their daddy. Molly and Magruder noticed a glittering sparkle light up the boys' eyes like blue stars. Everyone was happy to be home.

Made in the USA
Columbia, SC
13 December 2020

27875293R00031